The Sky Worm

Reading Practice

her
serve
nerve
stern
over
finger
singer

sir
girl
bird
first
stir
twirl
whirl

hurt
curl
turn
burn
lurch
disturb

word
world
worth
work
worm

earn
search
pearl
heard
early

Contents

Chapter 1	First Born	page 1
Chapter 2	Disturbing Bird	page 6
Chapter 3	Luring the Sky Worm	page 11
Chapter 4	All Over Now	page 15

Vocabulary

- blood-curdling – horrifying
- squealed – called out in surprise
- lurched – staggered or swayed
- panic – sudden fear or terror
- whimper – cry with a low, broken sound
- screeching – making a high-pitched scream
- urgently – insistently; conveying need for immediate attention
- surged – moved quickly and powerfully
- scamper – run quickly or playfully
- clambered – climbed using hands and feet
- emerged – came into view from being hidden
- scrambled – climbed quickly

Chapter 1: First Born

It was early the next day. Bain and Mina were fast asleep, curled up in the cave. Suddenly their sleep was disturbed by a blood-curdling scream! "What on earth is that?" squealed Mina. "Is it a bird? Is it hurt?"

They left the cave to go and search for the bird. They traveled a long way, leaving the snow way behind them. There was no bird to be seen. "What a way to wake up," grumbled Mina. "Maybe that scream was just a dream?"

Mina stretched her legs. Her foot knocked the green egg off Bain's back. It landed in the dirt. SMACK! Mina jumped down to pick it up. Cracks ran all over its surface. Was the baby dragon safe?

Suddenly the egg lurched in Mina's hands!

Mina and Bain gazed in wonder. First they saw a little green leg... then a tiny folded wing. Slowly a little baby dragon worked its way out of the broken egg shell!

"You're as green as a plate of peas," grinned Mina. "Let's name you Green."

Green stretched and giggled happily. He sniffed at the dirt and sneezed. Then he set off across the rocky path.

"I think he's keen to see the world!" said Mina.

Chapter 2: Disturbing Bird

Green was a quick learner and a very fast runner. He soon reached the edge of a steep cliff. Mina began to panic.
"Quick, Bain, we must catch up with him in case he falls over the top!"

Suddenly Green lurched back with a whimper. A massive bird whirled up in front of them, screeching in anger. It was a cross between a worm and a bird.

"It's a sky worm!" yelled Mina in terror.

She grabbed Green.

The angry sky worm hovered for a second and then left. What was it doing? Mina hugged Green close to her chest. She needed to keep him safe. "Let's go," she told Bain urgently. "I don't want to disturb that thing again!"

The gem began to glow. It had turned purple. Was there an egg close by?
Suddenly Bain grunted in panic. The sky worm was coming back! It surged up from the rocks below the cliff. Was it searching for them?

The sky worm hovered and then dropped back under the edge of the cliff. Green wriggled out of Mina's grip and chased the odd bird. Mina raced after him and saw him scamper to the edge of the cliff.

Chapter 3: Luring the Sky Worm

The sky worm was curled up on its nest. The purple dragon egg was under its belly! Mina spotted a boy standing in the shadows. He turned and grinned up at her. Mina and Bain clambered along the cliff, closer to the boy.

The boy ran over to them. He put his finger to his lips. He was making a trail of silver gems in the dirt. They twinkled in the sun. The sky worm lifted its head and spotted the gems. It liked things that glittered. It lurched after them.

Suddenly Green raced off! What was he doing? He scrambled up to the top of the sky worm's nest. The boy was waiting at the bottom of the slope. Green rolled the egg down to him. The sky worm heard him and it turned round!

"He's going to catch him!" screamed Mina. But Green was clever. He ran in circles round the bird. The bird twisted and turned, but the clever little dragon was always just out of reach! The sky worm began to get dizzy. Then he crashed down in the dirt.

Chapter 4: All Over Now

The boy emerged from the fog of dirt. Green was perched on his back and they were both grinning.

"I'm Nat," said the boy. "And this little dragon is amazing. That sky worm is too dizzy to stand up!"

They scrambled back up to the top of the cliff, leaving the dizzy bird collapsed on its nest. Green curled up and fell asleep on Nat's lap. "That was fun," said Nat. "I've been traveling alone for too long. Can I travel with you and help you with your search?"